H·E·B read 3

GROW YOUNG MINDS, READ 3 TIMES A WEEK

H-E-B is strongly committed to improving education in Texas and has supported Texas schools through the Excellence in Education Awards program for more than 10 years. In 2011, when H-E-B learned that Texas was facing a major challenge regarding early childhood education and kindergarten readiness, H-E-B started the Read 3 Early Childhood Literacy Campaign.

Read 3's goals are to provide easy and affordable access to books for Texas families and encourage families to read to their early learners at least three times every week. Reading to a child improves his literacy, and when a child's literacy improves, she is more likely to succeed in school, less likely to drop out, and more likely to finish college. That's a brighter future for the child, the family, and for Texas.

Commit to reading at least three times a week to your early learner. Take the Read 3 Pledge!

*"A, B, C and 1, 2, 3 – Reading is fun for me.
It helps me grow my young mind.
This week I pledge to read 3 times!"*

H-E-B está firmemente comprometido a mejorar la educación en Texas y ha apoyado a las escuelas de Texas a través del programa de Premios a la Excelencia en la Educación por más de 10 años. En 2011, cuando H-E-B se enteró de que Texas enfrentaba un desafío importante con respecto a la educación de la infancia temprana y la preparación para el jardín de niños, H-E-B comenzó la Campaña de Alfabetización de la Infancia Temprana de Read 3.

Los objetivos de Read 3 son proporcionar un acceso fácil y asequible a los libros para las familias de Texas y alentar a las familias a que lean a sus estudiantes que están en la infancia temprana por al menos tres veces a la semana. Leerle a un niño mejora su alfabetización y cuando la alfabetización de un niño mejora, es más probable que tenga éxito en la escuela, menos probabilidades de abandonarla y más probabilidades de terminar la universidad. Ese es un futuro más brillante para el niño, la familia y para Texas.

Comprométase a leer al menos tres veces por semana a su estudiante que está en la infancia temprana. ¡Tome la promesa de Read 3!

"A, B, C y 1, 2, 3 - La lectura es divertida para mí. Me ayuda a desarrollar mi mente joven. ¡Esta semana me comprometo a leer 3 veces!"

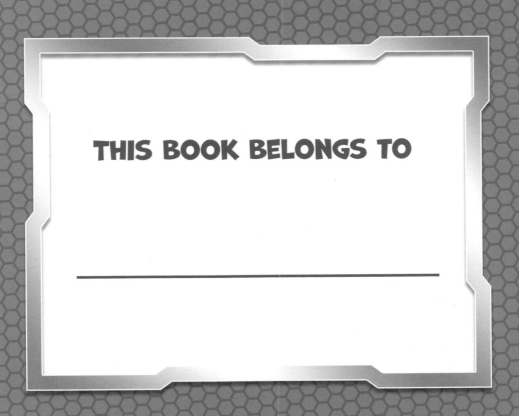

THIS BOOK BELONGS TO

_____

PUPS SAVE THE PARTY

One windy afternoon, the pups were in Katie's Pet Parlor, preparing a surprise birthday party for Chase.

"Streamers away!" said Rocky.

"Next up — the birthday cake!" said Katie.

"But who is making sure that Chase doesn't surprise us while we set up the surprise party?" asked Skye.

"Marshall," said Rubble. "He can keep a secret... can't he?"

Marshall and Chase played at the park. But Marshall was acting a little . . . different.

"Is something wrong, Marshall?"

"Wrong?" Marshall laughed nervously. "Why? It's not like I have a big secret I'm not supposed to tell . . ."

Just then, it got very windy!

"Maybe we should go find Ryder and the pups," said Chase.

"No! I mean, uh . . ." Marshall stammered. "It's so nice outside!"

Woosh! The wind got so strong that it blew the pups onto the swings . . . and onto the ground!

THUMP!

Back at the Pet Parlor, everyone was still busy getting ready for the party, when suddenly, the lights went dark and Katie's mixer stopped working.

"All the lights on the street are out, too," called Rocky. "What happened?"

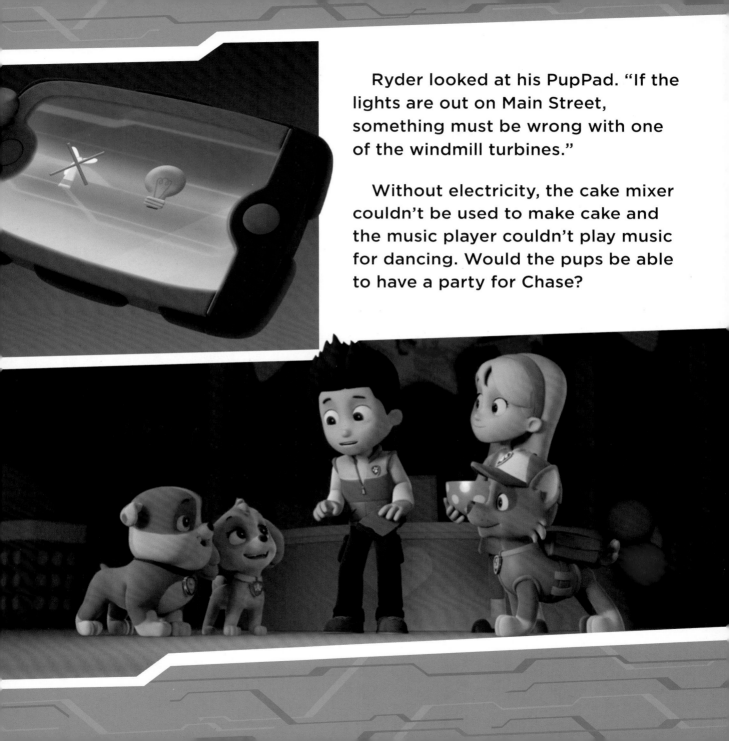

Ryder looked at his PupPad. "If the lights are out on Main Street, something must be wrong with one of the windmill turbines."

Without electricity, the cake mixer couldn't be used to make cake and the music player couldn't play music for dancing. Would the pups be able to have a party for Chase?

"We're going to throw Chase a party no matter what!" said Ryder, grabbing his PupPad. "PAW Patrol to the Lookout!"

The pups all raced to the Tower, but without electricity, the elevator wasn't working!

To figure out the problem, Ryder needed to get up to the Lookout. So Marshall got his truck and raised his ladder. Ryder climbed into the Lookout, looked through the periscope, and spotted the problem. The strong wind had broken a windmill blade and that's why there was no electricity.

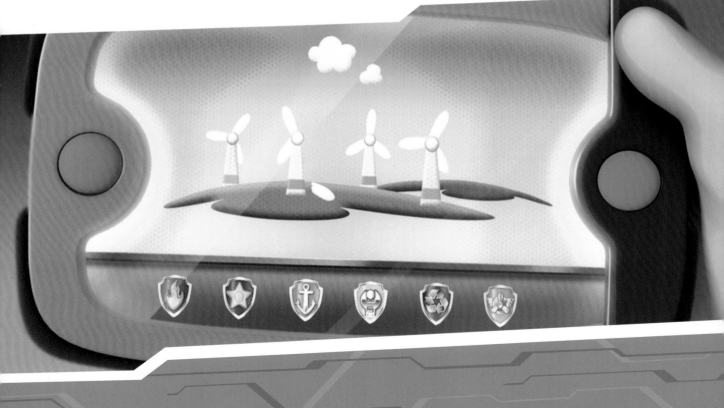

"Rocky," said Ryder, "I need you to find something in your truck to fix the broken blade."

"Marshall, we'll need your ladder to climb up and fix the windmill."

"Chase, the traffic lights won't work without electricity — we need your siren and megaphone to direct traffic."

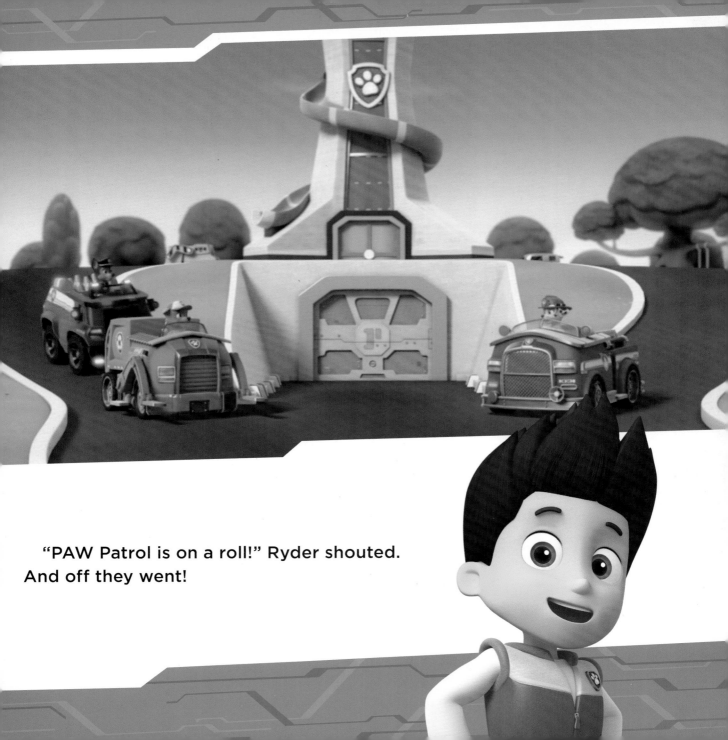

"PAW Patrol is on a roll!" Ryder shouted.
And off they went!

Skye, Rubble, and Zuma stayed behind at the Lookout.

"Time to save Chase's party!" said Skye.

"What are we going to do?" asked Zuma.

"We'll have a party in the dark!" said Rubble.

"Yeah! We'll give Chase the best surprise party in the dark, ever!" barked Skye.

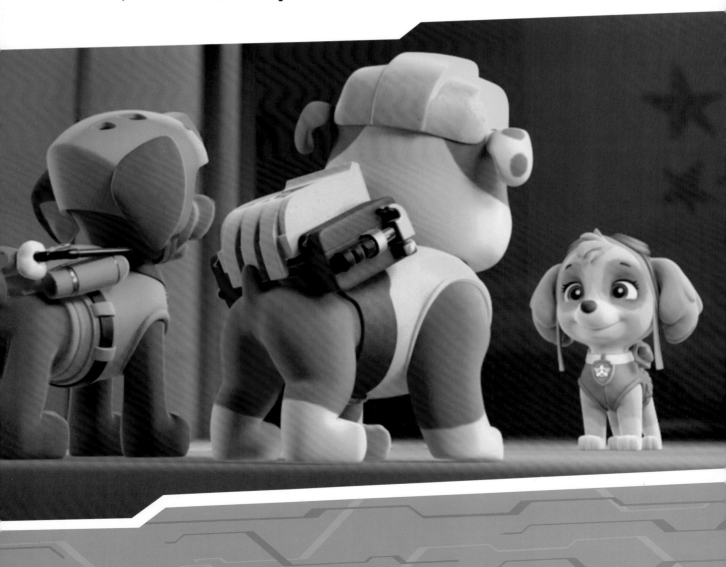

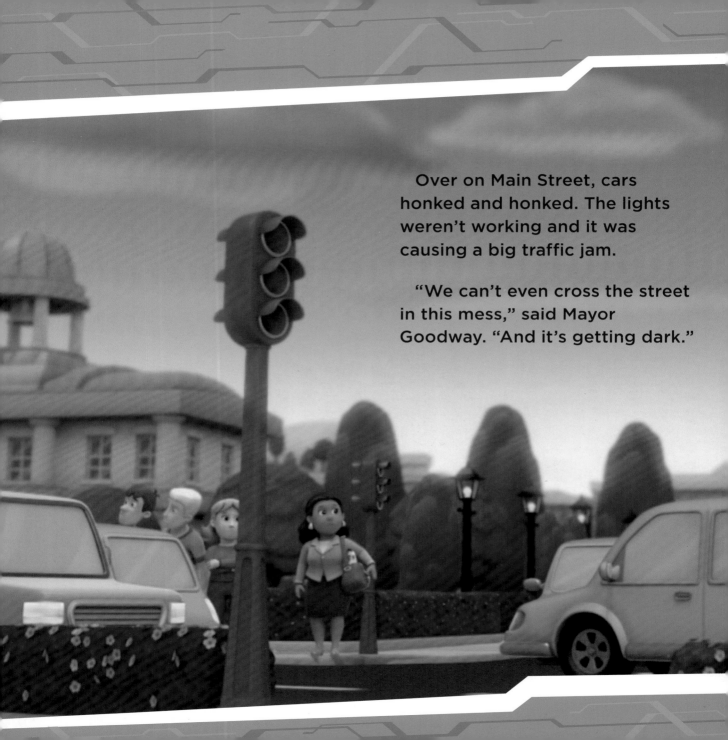

Over on Main Street, cars honked and honked. The lights weren't working and it was causing a big traffic jam.

"We can't even cross the street in this mess," said Mayor Goodway. "And it's getting dark."

Chase arrived and got straight to work with his megaphone.

"WOOF!" he barked. "Everyone going this way, go NOW! Okay, STOP!"

The drivers did as the police pup instructed and the traffic cleared. The road was safe to cross!

Meanwhile, Ryder, Marshall, and Rocky were busy fixing the windmill.

As Ryder climbed up Marshall's ladder and removed the broken blade, Rocky found the perfect thing to replace it. "Zuma's old surfboard!" said Rocky. "Why trash it when you can stash it?"

Ryder attached the surfboard to the windmill. It was perfect!

"This surfboard will catch a breeze," said Rocky, "and turn it into electricity!"

Back at the Pet Parlor, the pups were playing flashlight tag in the dark when the lights came back on. Ryder and the PAW Patrol did it!

"But there's no time to make a cake," said Skye.

"I have an idea," said Katie.

On Main Street, the traffic lights came back on.

"All right, everyone," Chase said in his megaphone. "It's safe to cross."

Everyone on Main Street thanked him!

Just then, Ryder called. "Chase. Change of plans. We need you at Katie's."

"On my way!" barked Chase.

Next, Ryder called Skye. "Chase is on his way and so are we!" he said.

"Great!" said Skye. "The surprise is all ready."

When Chase walked into Katie's Pet Parlor, all the lights were off.

"Hello," he called. "Anybody home?"

"SURPRISE!" everyone shouted, jumping out from behind the counter. "Happy Birthday, Chase!"

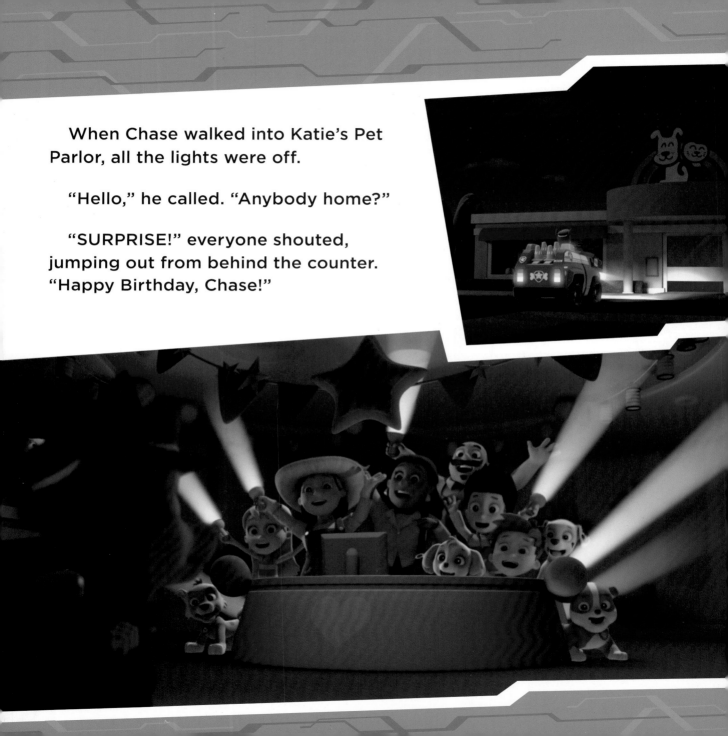

"You turned the lights back on _and_ made a party for me?" said Chase.

"Whenever it's your birthday, just yelp for help!" laughed Ryder.

"We couldn't make you a regular cake, so I hope you like your dog cookie cake," said Katie. "Make a wish!"

Chase blew out the candles, and then the pups helped him eat his birthday cake!